# Chubbs

## a blind cat learns to trust

A Story by Sandra Sorenson-Kindt  Illustrations by Sandra Jessop

LEAN IN PUBLISHING

With love
to my grandchildren
Grace, Matthew, Milly, Christian,
Robyn, and Julia…and those yet to come.
As you recognize God's Spirit in your life—
may you live courageously.


—Grandma Sandy

Chubbs's story begins the night Smooch disappeared...

Every evening after dinner, Smoochie loved to lounge on the neighbor's lawn. And every night before Grandma Sandy went to bed, she used her crazy cat voice to call Smooch home. But one summer night, she didn't come.

When the sun came up, Grandma looked around her house and knocked on her neighbors' doors, but Smoochie was nowhere to be found. So, Grandma pulled on some old hip boots and stomped through the muddy citrus groves. As she searched, an idea popped into her head—what if someone had taken Smooch to the pound?

Walking up and down the aisles at the pound, Grandma looked hopefully into each cage. After two loooong hours and one heavy sigh, she knew Smoochie was truly lost.

Maybe it was time for Grandma to find a new furry friend. She studied the cats again and narrowed her choice to two very different ones—a mangy alley cat with a magnificent, cloudlike tail and a prissy Persian with fluffy white fur and perfectly groomed nails.

Which cat would you pick?

The Persian princess appeared to be the "purrfect" choice, yet Grandma Sandy's heart nudged her to adopt the mangy one. It didn't make sense, but there was something special about Mangycat, and Grandma always trusted her feelings.

Have you ever had a feeling that you should
do something that didn't make sense?

The next morning, the vet checked out Grandma's new cat. Dr. Jack said she had a fever and ear mites, and that she only weighed six pounds. He gave her a shot but wasn't sure she'd get better.

Over the next week, Mangycat slept on a giant pile of towels in the laundry room. Grandma stayed close and prayed that her sick cat would get better.

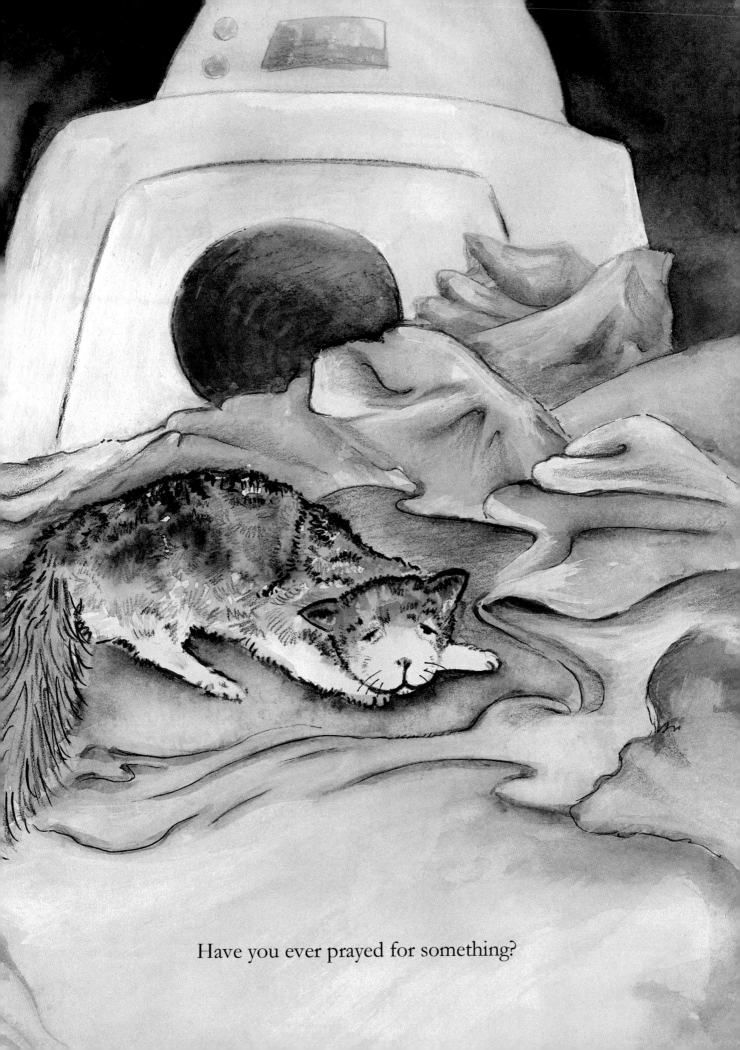

Have you ever prayed for something?

Grandma's prayer was answered. Mangycat grew strong enough to explore her new home. Inside, she found warm sunlit nooks perfect for napping. Outside, she found patches of rough gravel perfect for scratching her back. The newly cut grass must've smelled like catnip because she loved to nestle in it.

Mangycat grew round and healthy and transformed into Chubbs. The short, matted knots in her fur became a soft, beautiful coat. Petting her felt like stroking a bunny. Loud noises never bothered her. She came when she was called. And she was so chill that Grandma often teased Chubbs was really a dog stuck in a cat's body.

When two new kittens—Skid and Loverboy—moved in, Chubbs treated them like her babies. When Mama Chubbs put her big white paws around Skid's neck and licked her face and ears, she snuggled closer.

Loverboy didn't want another mama. He was happy being the "boss cat."

One day Grandma noticed that Chubbs's left eye was red and weepy. It quickly turned milky blue. Dr. Jack found thick cataracts—a cloudy film—that prevented her from seeing clearly. When the eye grew three times its normal size, it needed to be removed. Surgery frightened Grandma, but she loved Chubbs and wanted to do what was best for her. And she trusted Dr. Jack.

When you're scared, what do you do? How does it feel if someone you trust helps you?

The surgery went well. In no time, Chubbs strutted around as if she still had two eyes.

Years later, a blood clot got stuck in Chubbs's good eye, and it also needed to be removed. The first surgery had gone so well that Grandma wasn't as worried.

The night Chubbs came home, she woke up confused at 3:00 am yowling like an angry alley cat. Grandma Sandy jumped out of bed, scooped up her frightened cat and held her close, softly humming and whispering, "I got you, I got you, I got you," until Chubbs relaxed and fell asleep.

How do you feel when someone comforts you?

Losing both eyes turned Chubbs's world dark and small. She no longer explored the house, rolled in the gravel, smelled the grass, or scouted birds. She cried all the time and stayed close to Grandma.

Without her eyes, Chubbs had to learn to listen carefully. Familiar sounds—potato chips crunching, a soda can opening, someone talking, coughing, sneezing, or laughing—signaled that Grandma was nearby. Once Chubbs figured out where the sounds came from, she'd waddle toward them.

When she bumped into Grandma's feet, Chubbs perched her big self on top of them like a hen settling on a nest.

Chubbs's whiskers grew longer than usual, and she used them the way a blind person uses a cane. Slowly, she started exploring the house like her old confident self, using her instincts to avoid walls and furniture as if she had a built-in GPS.

Animals trust their instincts to survive. For instance, a cheetah can't always see other animals around her, but she knows they're there.

Sometimes we call instincts feelings. Unlike animals, who always listen to their instincts, we often ignore our feelings because they don't make sense or seem silly or unimportant.

Rather than ignoring the ideas that come to your mind or the feelings that come to your heart, what else could you do?

One day after breakfast, Chubbs headed from the kitchen to her bed—something she'd done a hundred times before. But this time, she circled round and round and round before turning toward the dining table where Loverboy crouched quietly in the dark, waiting for her to enter his lair.

Loverboy's fur blended into the earthy colors of the rug, but his amber eyes glowed like a campfire in the woods and gave away his hiding place to Grandma. She knew that by the time Chubbs walked into her brother's ambush, it would be too late. Grandma quickly called to Chubbs and made kissy noises. But she continued to creep toward Loverboy.

Growing more worried, Grandma began to snap. *Snap. Snap. Snap.* This time, Chubbs listened! She followed the snapping all the way to her bed.

Instead of snatching her up and carrying her away, Grandma waited to give Chubbs a chance to listen and follow the familiar sounds that signaled safety. God could "snatch" us up and remove us from danger or difficulty, but He gives us the chance to hear and follow His voice.

In a way, Grandma was Chubb's lifeguard. She saw danger when Chubbs couldn't. Most lifeguards sit in tall chairs to have a clear view of those who need help or those doing things that could put themselves or others in danger.

Would you like to have a lifeguard looking out for you?

Just as Grandma was Chubbs's lifeguard, God is our lifeguard. He watches over us, notices things sooner than we do, and recognizes danger when we don't. Chubbs couldn't "see" Grandma, and we can't see Him. But like Grandma stayed close to Chubbs, God's Spirit stays close to us even when we don't know it.

Chubbs spent her last
years in complete darkness,
bravely trusting her instincts
and Grandma Sandy to
protect her. We won't always
be able to see, control, or change
what will happen in our lives.
Sometimes we won't know which
way to go or what to do. But that's
okay. If we trust the ideas God puts in
our minds and the feelings He puts in our
hearts, we can make choices that will help us
live more courageously—just like Chubbs.

ISBN: 978-1-7347251-0-0 (Hardbound)
ISBN: 978-1-7347251-1-7 (Softbound)

Sandra Sorenson-Kindt, author
Chubbs: a Blind Cat Learns to Trust

An inspirational story about a blind cat who relies on Grandma Sandy for guidance and protection.

Library of Congress Control Number: 2020904272
Illustrations by Sandra Jessop
Editor: Lori Freeland
Digital Consultant: Steven Burger, Prodigitalimage
Layout and Design: Adrienne Quintana, Pink Umbrella Books

Made in the USA
Monee, IL
26 February 2023

28654044R10021